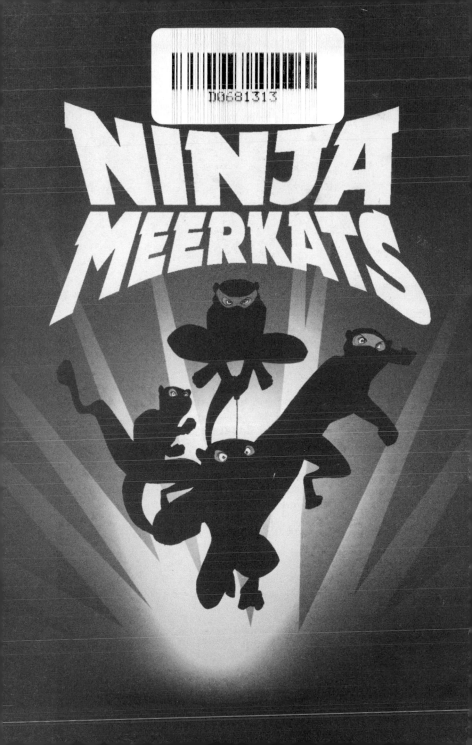

D0681313

# NINJA
## MEERKATS

## For Ethan Holt
### ~ G P J

SQUARE
FISH
An Imprint of Macmillan

Square Fish books may be purchased for business or promotional use.
For information on bulk purchases please contact the Macmillan Corporate
and Premium Sales Department at (800) 221-7945 x5442 or
by e-mail at specialmarkets@macmillan.com.

ISBN 978-1-250-02931-7 (paperback) / 978-1-250-04500-3 (ebook)

Originally published in Great Britain by Stripes Publishing
First Square Fish Edition: April 2013
Square Fish logo designed by Filomena Tuosto
mackids.com

2 4 6 8 10 9 7 5 3 1

# NINJA MEERKATS

# ESCAPE FROM ICE MOUNTAIN

## GARETH P. JONES

SQUARE
FISH

**NEW YORK**

Well, here we are again. Or at least, here I am. Precisely where you are, I cannot say, but I would hazard a guess that you are holding a book in your hands.

This is the story of my kidnapping and how I came to be rescued by the mighty Clan of the Scorpion. However, I am sorry to say that I am unable to recall a great many of the events featured in this tale. Apart from the fact that I spent a good deal of it asleep, my memory has gotten worse over the years. At least, I assume it used to be better but, to be honest, I cannot properly remember.

Even so, I could never forget the heroism of the Clan of the Scorpion: the team of four deadly ninja meerkats who risk their lives to keep the planet safe from the clutches of the Ringmaster—a villain intent on world domination.

In case you've been living under a rock and you need to be reminded, they are . . .

Jet Flashfeet: a super-fast ninja whose only fault is craving the glory he so richly deserves.

Bruce "the muscle" Willowhammer: the strongest of the gang, though in the brain race he lags somewhat behind.

Donnie Dragonjab: a brilliant mind, inventor, and master of gadgets.

Chuck Cobracrusher: his clear leadership has saved the others' skins more times than I care to remember.

And me? I'm Grandmaster One-Eye: as old and wise as the sand dunes themselves—even if my memory is a little hazy.

Even so, I can still recall a good many poems—such as this one, penned by the great enlightened thinker Claire Verclogs.

*Never pander to a panda,*
*and never bear a bear.*
*Avoid badgering a badger,*
*or hassling a hare.*
*If you seal a deal with a seal,*
*ensure it's sealed tight.*
*If you harangue an orangutan,*
*you'll end up in a fight.*

But now, it's time to settle down and enjoy the story of . . .

**ESCAPE FROM ICE MOUNTAIN.**

# CHAPTER ONE

## THE GRANDMASTERS' REUNION

The pilot of the twin-engine plane looked down at the Chilean mountain range. Even in the fading evening light, he could see all the way down to the southernmost tip of South America.

But what he failed to see were five small furry stowaways jumping out of his plane and parachuting down to earth. Chuck Cobracrusher, Donnie Dragonjab, Jet Flashfeet, and Bruce Willowhammer were all using parachutes designed by Donnie, with toggles on either side allowing them to steer.

Bruce was having the most difficulty, as he had their ancient mentor, Grandmaster One-Eye, strapped to his back.

"What are we aiming for?" shouted Jet, pulling his right toggle and swooping around in front of the others.

"The ground," smirked Donnie.

"We are aiming for the Academy of Revered Grandmasters, for Grandmaster One-Eye's school reunion," Chuck yelled over the sound of rushing wind.

"Did you really go to school here, Grandmaster?" asked Bruce.

Grandmaster One-Eye nodded.

"It seems like a long way to travel every day from the Red Desert," said Bruce.

"Bruce, the students who attend the ARG *live* at the academy," said Chuck.

"So, where is this place, Grandmaster?" asked Bruce. "I can't see it yet."

"I'm afraid I cannot see it either," replied One-Eye.

"Bruce, remember that Grandmaster One-Eye's eyesight is not as good as yours," Chuck pointed out.

"It isn't that," said One-Eye. "I've had my eyes shut since we jumped out of the plane. If meerkats were meant to see the world from such heights, they would have wings."

"My granddad had wings," said Bruce.

"No, he didn't," sighed Donnie.

"Yes, he did. I never saw them myself, but I remember Mom saying she wouldn't have him in the burrow because he had such a bad case of wings."

"I think that would have been *wind*," said Jet.

"Oh. That does make more sense now that you say it," admitted Bruce.

"Follow me," said Chuck,
pulling his toggles and aiming
for a spot near the top of a hill.
When he was moments from
the ground, he released the
parachute and landed into a roll.
The others followed suit, except
for Bruce, who took the force of
the landing in his knees to
avoid flattening Grandmaster
One-Eye. In front of them
were two large wooden
gates. A long golden rope
hung to one side.

"Ah, now this brings back memories," said Grandmaster One-Eye as Bruce set him on the ground. "Would you give me a moment before we go any farther?"

"You need time to reflect on all that has happened since you were last here?" said Chuck.

"No, I drank rather a lot of tea while we were waiting for that plane to take off and I need the bathroom," said Grandmaster One-Eye.

Jet chuckled and the Grandmaster disappeared into a nearby bush.

"Bruce, keep an eye on him," said Chuck.

"What? Watch him go to the toilet?" exclaimed Bruce.

"Yes. The last time he went, we lost him for an hour," replied Chuck.

"Don't worry," replied Donnie. "I've attached a tracking device to his robe so there's no chance of losing him again."

"I'm looking forward to getting inside and having some grub," said Bruce, carefully watching the bush Grandmaster One-Eye was hidden behind. "Oooh, I used to love school dinners. Mealworm mash, mealworm stew, mealworm Bolognaise . . ."

"We will not be entering the grounds," said Chuck. "According to ancient ninja code, no one is allowed to walk into the temple without an invitation."

"So, no mealworms?" said Bruce, disappointed.

"Not unless you find them yourself. We will set up camp nearby," said Chuck. "After the reunion, we will accompany Grandmaster One-Eye back home."

"I wish we could get inside and take a sneak peek," said Jet. "The ARG is the coolest academy in the world." He scurried onto a rock and jumped up, trying to see over the wall, but it was far too high.

"Please remove yourself from my shell," said a voice.

"Who said that?" asked Jet, spinning around.

"It was that rock you're standing on," said Donnie.

"That is no rock," said Chuck. "Jet, climb down at once."

Jet leaped off, and a small wrinkly head appeared from under what was in fact the shell of a giant tortoise.

"Professor Longtooth!" said Grandmaster One-Eye, reappearing from the bushes.

"Ah, young One-Eye."

"Young?" said Donnie, sniggering.

"Clan of the Scorpion, this is my old tutor, Professor Longtooth."

"Old is the right word," exclaimed Jet. "If you taught Grandmaster One-Eye you must be *ancient*!"

"I am old enough to remember when the young still showed their elders respect," said the professor. Jet bowed in apology.

"What are you doing out here, professor?" asked Grandmaster One-Eye.

"Do you know, I can't remember. I came out for something, then decided to have a little nap. When you get to my age there really is no substitute for a nap, you know."

"You must teach such awesome things in there," said Jet.

"Our students do not seek *awesome things*," scolded Professor Longtooth. "During their stay here they exist in peaceful isolation from the rest of the world, dedicating their minds and bodies to the study of kung fu."

"Except on Thursdays when they visit the local disco, as I recall," added Grandmaster One-Eye.

"Well, yes, Thursday night is disco night," said Professor Longtooth. "And on

Wednesdays we do knitting, of course."

"Knitting?" exclaimed Jet.

"Needlework involves the same principles
as kung fu," said the professor. "Precision,
timing, control . . . and an ability to not drop
stitches. Actually, I'm not sure about that
last one . . ."

"But when do they learn special
moves?" asked Jet. "They're the most
important thing! I'm working on the Single-
Claw Hole Punch at the moment. I can
almost get right through a tree trunk."

"In my class you would learn to punch
a hole through an entire mountain," said
the tortoise.

"Wow," exclaimed Jet, impressed.
"Would you teach me how to do that?"

"Perhaps one day I will. Right now, young
One-Eye needs to accompany me inside."
He turned to Grandmaster One-Eye. "Many

of the other masters are already here. Your old friend the Delhi Llama has been asking for you."

Professor Longtooth raised his long neck and, with his mouth, pulled on the rope by the side of the door. A gong sounded and the huge door creaked open. The party was already in full swing, and the aroma of delicious-smelling food wafted past.

"Can't we just pop in for a snack?" begged Bruce.

The tortoise slowly turned his head to face Bruce. "I'm afraid the rules are quite clear."

"I will bring you something tomorrow," said Grandmaster One-Eye, patting Bruce's paw comfortingly. "The academy's canteen does the best deep-fried lizards' tails."

"Deep-fried lizards' tails are my favorite," said Bruce wistfully.

Chuck, Donnie, Bruce, and Jet watched as the huge gates slammed shut behind One-Eye and Professor Longtooth.

"We should set up camp," said Chuck. "Come on."

They settled in a peaceful spot down the hill from the temple, by a stream. The trees were spaced farther apart here, allowing the meerkats to see the night sky.

"The perfect place for some tranquil meditation," said Chuck, sitting cross-legged on a rock and closing his eyes.

"I'll put up the tent," said Donnie.

He pulled a huge pop-up tent out of his backpack and set about banging pegs into the ground. Bruce noisily foraged for lizards and bugs, while Jet practiced his new move, closing his eyes and letting out a cry of "Eeeyah!" as he punched the trunk of a fallen tree, ripping a hole through the rotten wood.

"Do you all have to make so much noise?" Chuck sighed.

"At least I'm doing something useful—we need somewhere to sleep," said Donnie.

"And something to eat," said Bruce.

"And I need to practice the Single-Claw Hole Punch."

"But surely you do not need to make quite so much noise, Jet," said Chuck. "The Way of the Scorpion teaches us to—" He stopped mid-sentence.

"To what?" asked Jet.

"Balloon," said Chuck, pointing up.

"The Way of the Scorpion teaches us to *balloon*?" Bruce said.

"No, look." A large, round object was floating silently above them.

"It's a hot-air balloon," said Donnie. He shone his flashlight into the sky, illuminating the balloon. It was decorated in red and black stripes—identical in color to the Ringmaster's circus tent . . .

# CHAPTER TWO

## THE TRAINED TARANTULAS OF SANTIAGO

"Looks like we have an unwelcome visitor—but what is the Ringmaster after this time?" Chuck wondered, as the hot-air balloon drifted directly above the temple. "Clan of the Scorpion, we must alert the grandmasters." They scrambled up the hill and Donnie pulled the golden rope, but the noise from the party drowned out the gong. Bruce tried to shoulder the door, but it wouldn't budge.

"What now? These walls are far too high to jump over, even if we used the Helicopter Leap," said Jet.

"Wait, I have just the thing," said Donnie. He unfolded a device from his backpack that consisted of a long stick with a spring at one end and propellers at the other.

"I call it the Elephant's Pullover," announced Donnie.

"Why's that?" asked Bruce.

"Because it's a *really big sweatshirt.* D'you get it? Because an elephant's pullover is like a really big sweatshirt?"

Bruce frowned. "Nope, I don't get it. How does it work?"

"I'll show you. Take hold of the handle," Donnie told them, as he pulled back the spring. "This thing's got quite a kick."

He
flicked a
catch,
releasing
the spring
and sending the pole flying
into the air. The propellers spun
faster and faster.

"Whoooah!" cried Bruce, as they
soared high above the temple walls and
past the hot-air balloon.

"Sorry! Think I overshot," Donnie
shouted over the sound of the whirring
propellers.

In the courtyard, ancient lemurs, llamas,
monkeys, mongooses, and other animal
species were sitting at a large banquet
table. In spite of their age, all were
behaving like giddy teenagers, unaware
of what was happening above.

Slowly, Donnie's device brought them down, level with the basket hanging below the hot-air balloon. Inside, seven identically dressed siblings jostled for space.

"It's the Von Trapeze family," said Jet. "We can handle these flying siblings, no problem."

"It's those miserable meerkats!" exclaimed the eldest Von Trapeze boy.

"They're not our only problem," said Chuck. "Look."

Underneath the basket hung a number of fine threads. Large, sinister-looking black spiders were rapidly descending toward the party below.

"I'll burst the balloon, and you three head to the banquet and stop the spiders," cried Chuck. He drew his sword and leaped into the air. But the Von Trapeze children were one step ahead. Suddenly, the balloon

shot upwards, and Chuck's perfectly aimed
leap fell short. He crashed down to the
banquet table below. Moments later, Donnie,
Jet, and Bruce landed beside him, sending
bowls and goblets flying into the air.

"What's the meaning of this?"
demanded Professor Longtooth.

"Grandmasters, you're under
attack!" shouted Chuck.

One of the spiders landed directly in
front of the meerkats and instantly sprang
up into a spinning attack. Jet ducked as
another spider flew past. Quick as a flash,
Donnie grabbed a teapot, lifted the lid, and
caught the spider inside.

"And he's not itsy-bitsy enough to
climb up the spout either," said Donnie.

"I've heard of spiders spinning webs,
but not *themselves*," said Bruce.

"These are the Trained Tarantulas
of Santiago!" cried Professor
Longtooth. "Deadly assassins for hire."

"Don't worry, we'll deal with them,"
said Jet, drawing his nunchucks.

Bruce cracked his knuckles, and Donnie
pulled out a rolled-up newspaper.

"What's that for?" asked Bruce.

"You know a better way of dealing with spiders?" replied Donnie.

But before they could leap into action, several spiders flew over their heads and splatted into a wall.

"Look—the grandmasters are fighting back," said Chuck.

"And they've got some moves too," added Jet. "Old school Ninja-boom!"

An ancient porcupine was executing a perfect roundhouse kick; a decrepit badger was plucking spiders out of the air and bowling them at Smo Ka, the Delhi Llama, who was hoofing them away as though it were a game. Even Professor Longtooth was helping by swatting the spiders off course with his long claws.

"Looks like they don't need us after all," said Bruce.

"I don't understand," said Jet. "Why would the Ringmaster send a group of trained assassins to attack these old-timers?"

"The spiders are a distraction," said Chuck. "I think the real villains are up there."

The meerkats watched as the Von Trapeze family formed a human ladder down from the basket of the balloon.

"We must stop them," said Chuck.

They made their way as fast as they could across the courtyard, dodging flying spiders and lunging grandmasters.

The chain of trapeze artists touched the ground but, with the chaos of the battle, by the time the meerkats reached them, it was too late.

"I've got him!" shouted the young acrobat at the bottom.

Only as they began to climb back up did it become apparent *whom* they had got.

"It's Grandmaster One-Eye!" cried Donnie, spotting their mentor struggling to free himself.

A burst of flame sent the balloon back up into the night sky. The meerkats watched helplessly as their old friend and master was passed up the line and into the basket.

# CHAPTER THREE

## A SHIP SOUTH

As the balloon climbed into the sky, the tarantulas scurried away.

"The Trained Tarantulas of Santiago are retreating," cried Professor Longtooth.

"Try saying that after two sticks of sugar cane," chuckled the Delhi Llama.

"Professor Longtooth," said Chuck, "while we were kept busy with the spiders, I'm afraid our enemy the Ringmaster's henchmen kidnapped Grandmaster One-Eye!"

"What?" said the professor. "Then we will follow them!"

The huge tortoise moved one of his feet, then another, slowly making his way after the balloon.

"Forgive me, Professor Longtooth," said Chuck. "I think this may be a task for younger and . . . *ahem* . . . faster feet."

"You are probably right," said the wrinkly-faced old tortoise. "And I could do with a little nap after all this excitement."

Chuck bowed, then turned to Donnie. "Is that tracking device still working?"

Donnie pulled out his phone. "It's coming through loud and clear."

"Then let's go," said Chuck.

"Jet Flashfeet, a word before you depart," said Professor Longtooth. He raised his long neck and whispered something in Jet's ear. Jet listened carefully, then nodded and bowed before leaving with the others.

● ● ●

Through the night, the meerkats traveled on foot over the mountains, following the signal from Donnie's phone.

After several hours, they reached the top of a peak, where they could see the ocean stretching out before them. As dawn broke, the hot-air balloon was no more than a tiny speck just above the horizon.

"It's heading south," said Chuck. "And there is only one thing in that direction. The Antarctic."

"Is that the one with penguins or polar bears? I can never remember," asked Bruce.

"Penguins. Polar bears live in the Arctic," replied Chuck.

"Shame. I'd like to meet a polar bear."

"This isn't a visit to the zoo, Bruce!" Jet exclaimed. "The Ringmaster has kidnapped Grandmaster One-Eye!"

"I wonder what he wants with him?" Donnie pondered.

"Grandmaster One-Eye has a great knowledge of the ways of kung fu and he knows many secrets that would interest the Ringmaster," Chuck pointed out.

"I wish him luck trying to get any sense out of him," said Donnie.

"Donnie, you should show more respect

for our master. Now, do you have anything that will enable us to follow them across the ocean?"

"Nothing that would survive the journey," replied Donnie. He pulled out his binoculars. "But there's a city on the coast down there that I think must be Punta Arenas. That's where most research trips set off for the Antarctic from, so with any luck, we'll be able to find a boat heading south."

"How do you know that?" asked Jet.

Donnie rolled his eyes. "Am I the *only* one who reads the guidebooks before going places?"

Chuck and Jet looked embarrassed, but Bruce said, "I read a guidebook in that café at the airport."

"That was a menu," sighed Donnie.

"Oh. That explains why there was such a big section on food," said Bruce.

"Donnie, your dedication humbles us all," said Chuck, bowing. "Now let us go and find transportation."

They hurried down to the city as fast as they could and made their way to the port.

"How do we tell which boat is going to the Antarctic?" asked Jet.

"We could ask those dogs," said Bruce.

Sitting by the side of a road were two huskies.

"Excuse me, do you know of a ship going to the Antarctic?" asked Chuck.

"All those ships will cross the ocean to the Antarctic at some point," said the larger of the dogs, a sad look in his eyes.

"Excellent, because we are looking to hitch a ride," said Chuck.

"Hitch a ride?" said the other dog. "They can't hitch a ride, can they Harold? They're not indigenous."

"What does that mean?" asked Bruce.

"It means meerkats don't live in the Antarctic," Donnie explained.

"Exactly," snapped the second dog. "If we're not allowed to go, then I can't see why they should be allowed to."

"Come now, Hilda, there's no need to take our frustrations out on strangers," said Harold. "Don't mind her. She gets a bit upset because we both come from a long line of Antarctic huskies, you see."

"That's right," said Hilda. "My parents, my grandparents, my great-grandparents, my great-great—"

"I think they get the idea, my darling,"

said Harold, patting her paw soothingly.
"Anyway, the humans changed the rules
some time ago. No more non-indigenous
animal species are allowed into Antarctica,
and that means no huskies."

"So your families were made to leave?"
asked Jet.

"Yes! I . . . I . . ." Hilda croaked, trying to
speak as her eyes filled with tears.

"What's wrong with her?" Bruce asked.

"She's probably just feeling a bit husky,"
Donnie replied. "D'ya get it? Feeling a bit
*husky*?"

"Donnie," said Chuck sternly. "This is
no time for jokes." He turned to address
the dogs. "Please, good huskies, our dear
friend has been kidnapped and taken
south. We must find transportation to
Antarctica. Do you know which boat we
can stow aboard?"

Harold paused for a moment. "Just because we can't go, it doesn't mean we should stand in the way of your rescue mission. That boat down there is the next to leave for the South Pole." He nodded in the direction of a large steel boat at the end of a nearby pier. "But you'd better get going. It's about to set off."

"You have our deepest thanks," said Chuck, bowing.

The meerkats made it on board just in time, unnoticed by the crew as they scurried up a gangway and snuck inside one of the lifeboats on deck.

"We're a long way behind the balloon now," said Donnie, checking Grandmaster One-Eye's signal on his phone.

"Then we will have the element of surprise on our side," said Chuck. "The Ringmaster will not anticipate us following them at all."

"I hope Grandmaster's OK," said Bruce.

"He'll be fine," said Jet. "He's tougher than he looks. He told me he was once kidnapped by the Seven Samurai Snails and held in a location high in the Himalayas, and yet he still managed to escape and find his way home in time for tea."

"How did he manage that?" asked Bruce.

Jet smirked. "Apparently they left a trail."

# CHAPTER FOUR

## THE TUXEDO TEN

The journey across the ocean felt as if it lasted much longer than four days. Bruce was seasick the whole way, which was no fun for the others since they all had to remain in the lifeboat to avoid being spotted.

"I'm bored," moaned Jet. "Why can't I have a run around on deck? Just for a minute? I'll be so quick the researchers won't even notice me—promise."

"Jet, like a mouse in a house full of cats, it is best to remain hidden," replied Chuck.

When the boat eventually arrived at the research base—a large orange building on stilts (and the only thing with any color for miles around)—the meerkats watched from the safety of the lifeboat as the researchers pulled sleds laden with equipment through a heavy  snowstorm. Once everything had been unloaded, the researchers hurried inside the base to escape the freezing temperatures.

"How far away is Grandmaster One-Eye, Donnie?" asked Chuck.

Donnie checked his phone. "About twenty miles up the coast," he replied.

"Twenty miles!" exclaimed Jet. "How are we going to get that far without freezing our tails off?"

"Yeah, if I'd known we were going somewhere this cold I'd have packed my thermal jumpsuit," said Bruce.

"A well-trained ninja should adapt to his surroundings like the chameleon adapts to his," said Chuck. "We have no choice but to brave this weather on foot."

"I've got an idea," said Donnie, pulling a screwdriver from his backpack. "You see that sled the researchers were using? Jet and Chuck, bring it over here. Bruce, you come with me."

Chuck and Jet climbed out of the lifeboat and dropped to the deck, then scampered down the gangway off the boat. It was snowing so heavily that their fur was instantly covered in a sheet of white. They scuttled over to the research base, grabbed the sled, and dragged it back.

"This thing is heavy," grumbled Jet.

"The smallest ant can pull the largest rock so long as there is an end in— Watch out!" cried Chuck. He leaped forward and pushed Jet out of the way, as a lifeboat motor fell from above and landed precisely where Jet had been standing.

"Sorry!" yelled Bruce. "Didn't see you down there."

Donnie and Bruce joined the others, and Donnie hammered the motor to the back of the sled.

"We must return these things when our mission is complete," Chuck reminded him.

"Right, we're all set," said Donnie. He looked up at the sky. "Good thing the snowstorm is letting up—that'll make it easier to navigate. Everyone on board—I'll steer."

The others climbed on to the sled and Donnie pulled the starter cable. The engine roared to life and the sled shot forward at an alarming speed.

"This should help us catch up," Donnie shouted over the noise of the engine. He checked his phone to make sure they were heading in the right direction.

"We should approach more quietly—the Way of the Scorpion teaches us that a ninja must tread lightly and silently, as the insect on the surface of the water," said Chuck.

"What did you say?" yelled Donnie.

"He said something about being nervous of the water," cried Jet.

"Who's got a thermos of water?" asked Bruce.

"*Penguins*!" Chuck yelled suddenly.

"Penguins?" bellowed Donnie.

"Penguins!" cried Jet.

"Why do you all keep saying 'penguins'?" asked Donnie.

Suddenly he saw what all the fuss was about. Blocking their way were ten Emperor penguins standing to attention, a threatening look in their eyes. He cut the engine, but there was no way the sled was going to stop in time.

"Get out of the way!" shouted Donnie.

At the last minute, the penguins moved aside, revealing a sudden drop behind them.

"Abandon sled!" yelled Chuck.

The meerkats leaped from the speeding sled. It careened over the edge of the cliff and crashed down into the valley below.

"That wasn't our sled," groaned Chuck. "We were just borrowing it."

"Oh, dear. Shouldn't have driven it off that cliff then, should they, Mr. White?" smirked the largest penguin.

The penguin next to him chuckled. "No, they shouldn't have, Mr. Black."

"The question is, why are they here, Mr. Gray?" said Mr. Black.

"They're here to upset the natural equilibrium of our delicate ecosystem, thereby putting our survival at considerable risk, Mr. Black."

The other penguins turned to look at him.

"They're here to make trouble," said Mr. Gray.

The other penguins nodded vigorously and made a loud trumpeting noise in agreement.

"We have no quarrel with you," said Chuck. "We simply want to pass."

"Huddle, boys," said Mr. Black.

The penguins waddled in close and put their heads together. The meerkats could hear the low sound of their muttered conversation, but couldn't make out what they were saying.

"Why are we wasting our time with these birds?" asked Jet.

"We are on their territory," said Chuck. "We must show them respect."

"I'll show them some Bruce Force in a minute," muttered Bruce.

The penguins finished their conversation and reformed the line. "After discussion with my colleagues," said Mr. Black, "we have decided you might be seal spies and therefore you will not be allowed to pass."

"Seal spies?" exclaimed Jet. "Do we look like seals?"

"I like seals," said Bruce.

"As we suspected," said Mr. White. "Get them, boys."

"Bruce!" exclaimed Chuck. "That wasn't especially helpful."

Bruce shrugged. "I just mean I saw some at a water park once. They were balancing balls on their noses. They were cool!"

The penguins dived onto their bellies and slid along the icy ground toward the Clan with terrifying speed, their sharp beaks aimed right at them.

Jet drew his nunchucks, Bruce raised his fists, and Donnie grabbed a smoke grenade in each hand.

"Clan of the Scorpion, you may defend yourselves, but do not harm these penguins," Chuck warned.

"But they're attacking us," protested Jet, swinging his nunchucks.

Chuck drew his sword. "Remember, we are the intruders here."

Jet jumped over one of the penguins and holstered his nunchucks. The others executed similar evasive moves, but the birds were swift to alter their course with a twitch of the tail, using their short wings to guide them.

"How are we supposed to defend ourselves if we can't fight?" asked Bruce.

"By using your environment," said Chuck.

Three penguins zoomed toward him. Chuck stood as still as a statue, then, at the last moment, he jumped into the air and somersaulted out of the way. The penguins crashed into a mound of snow, bringing a small avalanche down on their heads.

Chuck landed next to the other meerkats. "Do you get my drift?"

The Clan of the Scorpion were now standing with their backs to each other, while the penguins surrounded them.

"Please, stop—we mean you no harm!" shouted Chuck.

"Oh, really? Well, maybe this will remind Colonel Ron that next time he sends his spies, he should remember who he's dealing with," said Mr. Black.

"Yeah, a ten-strong unit of Emperor penguins dedicated to the protection and preservation of their natural environment!" said Mr. Gray.

The other penguins looked at him.

"He means we are the Tuxedo Ten," said Mr. White.

A loud trumpeting sounded the others' agreement.

"We don't know who Colonel Ron is," said Donnie.

"That's exactly what we'd expect you to say, isn't it, boys?" said Mr. Black.

The penguins edged forward menacingly.

"What's the plan?" asked Jet.

"Leave this to me," said Bruce, clenching his fists. "I've had one of my ideas."

"Don't, Bruce!" cried Chuck.

But it was too late. Bruce thumped the ground with both fists, sending shockwaves rippling across the snow. The next moment, a distant rumbling began, growing louder and louder.

"Avalanche!" Jet cried, pointing to the wave of white rushing toward them, down a nearby slope. "Get out of here!"

With incredible agility, all four meerkats leaped out of the way, but the penguins couldn't avoid being buried in several tons of fresh snow.

"Come on," said Chuck, dusting himself off. "Our penguin pursuers will be free in no time. And we must not forget our goal— to rescue Grandmaster One-Eye!"

# CHAPTER FIVE

## THE SEAL ARMY

There is a very good reason you don't find meerkats in the Antarctic. They don't like the cold. While their fur provides protection in the desert on a cold night, it isn't designed for the harsh environment of the South Pole.

"I've never been so c-c-cold in my l-l-life," stammered Bruce.

"Our suffering is nothing compared to what the Ringmaster is likely to be putting Grandmaster One-Eye through," said Chuck. "We must make haste."

The Clan of the Scorpion climbed over

hills and through valleys. The wind picked up, sending powdery snow into their faces. Eventually, the signal on Donnie's phone led them to a cave entrance at the base of an icy mountain. Outside, the red and black balloon was tethered to the ground.

"According to the signal, he's inside the mountain," said Donnie.

"We must stay close to one another," warned Chuck, as he led the way into the cave. "We may have the benefit of surprise on our side, but we have no idea what lies within the mountain, or what has happened to Grandmaster One-Eye."

A series of icy tunnels led deep into the
belly of the mountain. Wherever the tunnels
presented them with a choice of paths, they
used the flashing red signal on Donnie's
phone to work out which way to go. They
had just set off down a fairly narrow tunnel
when they heard a rumbling sound.

"Hungry, Bruce?" said Jet.

"That wasn't my stomach," said Bruce.

"No, it's coming from above," said Chuck.

The sound grew louder. The ground
began to shake. A large chunk of ice fell
from the ceiling.

"The tunnel's collapsing," cried Donnie.
"Move!"

The meerkats dived and rolled out of
the way, just in time to avoid being crushed.

A thundering sound echoed off the walls and clouds of snow billowed through the tunnel. Donnie stood up and brushed himself off.

"That was close," he said.

No one replied.

"Guys?" He spun around. A wall of ice and snow blocked the tunnel. The others were nowhere to be seen. Donnie pulled out his phone and dialed Chuck's number.

"Donnie! Are you all right?" Chuck answered.

"I'm fine. Is everyone else OK?"

"Yes, but there is no way through to you. Jet just tried to make a hole using his Single-Claw Hole Punch and almost brought the rest of the tunnel down on top of us. The mountain is very unstable."

"And I think I know why," said Donnie.

"Hold on." He pulled out a small drill and made a series of holes in the ground. Then he shone a flashlight into the holes.

"What are you doing?" asked Chuck.

"I'm analyzing the mountain. It's not just icy because it's cold. The whole thing is actually made of solid ice."

"So the whole mountain is about as stable as an ice-cream sundae on a skateboard," Chuck replied. "We must proceed in haste. How can we get to you?"

"Don't worry about me. If you follow the tunnel you're in, you'll be heading toward Grandmaster One-Eye. I'll find another way around," Donnie assured him.

"As fast as you can, please," said Chuck. "I have a feeling this mountain is likely to be full of unpleasant surprises."

Donnie continued on alone, following Grandmaster One-Eye's signal. After a few wrong turns and dead ends he finally managed to head in the right direction, but his route had sent him a long way around. As he scurried down a twisty tunnel, he suddenly heard voices shouting.

"One, two, one and two . . . Ready, aim . . . fire!"

The shouts were followed by loud crashes, and were coming from the other side of an arched doorway. Donnie crept through it and hid behind a ridge of ice. He gawked at the sight in front of him. He was in a huge ice hall, filled with hundreds of large gray seals covered in black spots. Some were marching up and down. Some were leaping through hoops, others were perfecting their pole vaulting. In one corner, a group were practicing a form of martial arts.

It was basic in style, mostly involving slapping each other with their flippers, but it looked pretty effective. In another corner, a line of seals was balancing balls of solid ice on their noses. On the command "Fire!", they flung the balls at a line of crudely made snowmen, knocking their heads clean off. Another seal was rebuilding the heads, hastily patting the snow down with its flippers, while trying to avoid getting hit by the flying ice balls.

Donnie pulled out his phone and called Chuck.

"I've found those seals the penguins mentioned," Donnie whispered.

"What are they like?" asked Chuck.

Another ice ball flew across the hall, pulverizing a snowman's head.

"I wouldn't want to meet them in a dark alley . . . or in a tunnel of an ice mountain, for that matter," said Donnie. "It seems to be some kind of army training camp."

"Can you keep watch while we rescue Grandmaster One-Eye? There's a good chance the Ringmaster could be—"

The phone went dead.

"Chuck?" said Donnie. He tried again and went straight through to Chuck's voicemail.

"This is Chuck's phone," said Chuck's voice. "Like an escapologist in the middle of a trick, I am tied up and unable to get to the phone right now. Please leave a message after the tone."

"Right, you 'orrible lot, jump to attention!" a voice cried from inside the hall.

Donnie peeked over the ridge and saw two seals waddling through the hall. One wore a red beret and bellowed at the others to get a move on, while the second was older and had long whiskers.

The rest of the seals quickly stopped what they were doing and formed a line.

Some of them snarled at each other angrily as they got in one another's way.

"Settle down, settle down!" cried the large seal with the beret. "Colonel Ron wishes to speak."

There was a hush in the hall.

"Friends, leopard seals, Antarcticans," said the older one. "Who is your leader?"

"Colonel Ron, Colonel Ron!" chanted the army of seals.

The old seal smiled. "We leopard seals are naturally the strongest, the toughest, and the deadliest seals in the whole world."

The army erupted into applause.

"And only one band of rebel penguins stands in the way of us controlling this whole area—the Tuxedo Ten."

The seals honked angrily.

"As you know, we have sealed a deal to ensure we crush these penguins for good. And to fulfill our part of the deal, I need a very special task force." He turned to the big seal next to him and said, "Sergeant, I need your twenty best soldiers."

The sergeant shuffled along the lines. The seals jostled for position, eager to be picked.

"You lot come with me," said Colonel Ron, once the twenty were assembled. "Everyone else, evacuate Ice Mountain."

Such was the rush for the exit that Donnie had to burrow into the ice to hide and only narrowly avoided being crushed by stampeding seals.

# CHAPTER SIX

## UNDERGROUND AMBUSH

While Donnie hid from the seals, Chuck, Bruce, and Jet were facing a far bigger problem. Chuck's phone had been swiped from his paw by a huge white bear, who'd appeared out of nowhere. It smashed the phone against the wall, cutting the line dead. Before Chuck could say, "A polar bear in the Antarctic?" the bear wrapped a large paw around the meerkat's waist, pinning his arms to his sides, and squeezed as hard as he could. Chuck struggled to reach his sword, but the bear's grip was too tight.

"Ninja-boom!" cried Jet, drawing his nunchucks. He somersaulted through the air, hurling himself at their attacker, but the bear landed a powerful punch on Jet's chest with his free paw, sending him flying backwards.

"Bruce Force!" cried Bruce. He leaped forward too, but was brought down by a flurry of snowballs from behind.

Jet pulled Bruce to his feet.

"Hey, Barnie, that was a bit of a *frosty* reception you gave them," said a voice.

"Nah, looks like Barnie's got a *crush* on Cobracrusher," said another.

"The ... clowns ..." said Chuck, gasping for breath.

Jet and Bruce spun around to see their old enemies Grimsby and Sheffield carrying handheld cannons. A barrage of snowballs flew at them, knocking the two meerkats off their feet and sending them into an icy wall.

"Mind you, Grimsby, looks like they're *bowled over* to see us."

The clowns laughed and fired two more rounds of snowballs. But this time, Jet and Bruce were ready for them. They leaped into the air, shattering the snow missiles with lightning-quick moves, spraying snow everywhere.

"Is that all you clowns have got, some oversized snowballs?" cried Jet. "This is going to be easy!"

"I wouldn't be so sure," said Grimsby, wearing a cruel smile beneath his sad painted face. "Don't forget Barnie, the *bear*-knuckle fighter. He already seems to have taken a shine to your leader!"

"Polar . . . bears . . . don't live in . . . the Antarctic," said Chuck, struggling to breathe as Barnie held him tight.

The clowns laughed and fired more snowballs. "He doesn't *live* here. He's on holiday. And we've come to help get rid of a penguin problem," said Sheffield.

"The penguins . . . have every right . . . to live here," gasped Chuck.

"You should spend less time worrying about those flightless birds and more time worrying about the fact that you're soon to be extinct," said Grimsby.

"And that's *snow* joke," added Sheffield. ·

"Nice one, lad," said Grimsby.

"Finding it . . . hard to . . . breathe," gasped Chuck. "Jet . . . Bruce . . . I could do . . . with some . . . help . . . here. Use my . . . sword."

"Bruce—distract the polar bear," whispered Jet.

Bruce nodded and turned to face the bear. "Right, Barnie, if that's your name, let's see what you can do."

The bear growled and stepped forward. Jet launched himself at Barnie, silently clambered up his side, scurried down his arm, and pulled Chuck's sword from its sheath. But the clowns were watching every move and opened fire with another volley of snowballs, knocking Jet flying and throwing Bruce to the ground. As Jet landed, he caught Barnie's foot with the edge of Chuck's sword.

The bear roared in pain and threw Chuck at a wall. Chuck slid to the ground in a crumpled heap.

"Are you OK?" asked Jet.

Chuck sat up. "I feel like an orange at breakfast time . . ." he said. "Squeezed and drained."

The clowns laughed.

"I don't see what's so funny," Bruce snarled.

"You need to chill out," said Sheffield.

"Hey, Grimsby, I think snow's forecast again."

"How lovely. What time?"

"About now."

Both clowns aimed their guns at the ceiling and fired. There was a loud crack, followed by boulders of ice falling on top of them. Jet and Bruce grabbed Chuck and dived to safety.

When the air cleared a moment later, the meerkats found themselves on the other side of the avalanche from Sheffield, Grimsby, and Barnie.

"Come back, you cowards!" cried Bruce, leaping to his feet.

"I have a bad feeling about this," said Chuck. "There must be a reason why they want us on this side of the avalanche. Quick, we must find Grandmaster One-Eye and get out of here right away."

"Perhaps Donnie's found him," said Jet, handing Chuck his sword.

"We were cut off when the bear attacked and destroyed my phone," said Chuck. "Bruce, call him on yours."

Bruce pulled out his phone, set it to loudspeaker and dialed the number.

"Bruce! What happened to you guys?" whispered Donnie.

"We had a run-in with our favorite clowns and their pet polar bear," said Bruce. "But it was nothing we couldn't handle."

"Donnie, what have you found out?" Chuck interrupted.

"Most of the seals were told to evacuate. But a team of twenty were picked for a special squad—I'm following them at the moment. They're up to something, but I'm not quite sure what—"

There was a crackling sound on the line, then a cold voice, dripping with evil, spoke. "Would you like me to tell you what it is?"

"The Ringmaster!" exclaimed Jet.

"Indeed, Flashfeet. I hope you don't mind me tapping into your phone call. Sorry if the line isn't very good. I'm quite a long way away."

There was an eager barking on the Ringmaster's end of the phone.

"Doris says hello," said the Ringmaster.

"What do you want? Why have you kidnapped Grandmaster One-Eye?" demanded Chuck.

"Oh, dear. Haven't you worked that out yet? To entice you into my trap, of course."

"What trap?" demanded Chuck.

"Oh, it's painfully simple. Painful for you, that is. As we speak, Colonel Ron's seal army is planting a series of snow explosives in these tunnels. When they go off, they will bring the whole mountain down. Not even you, my small burrowing friends, will be able to survive an entire mountain collapsing on top of you. And I will be free of your meddlesome ways once and for all."

"Why are you telling us this?" said Donnie.

"Because you still have to find your flaky master. You won't leave him to die, will you? Of course you won't. Your over-confidence and loyalty are your weaknesses and will be the end of you."

"Donnie, you have to stop the seals planting the explosives," said Chuck.

Another laugh crackled down the line.

"I'm afraid that even Donnie and his famous bag of gadgets will be helpless against Colonel Ron's seal army. If you had the element of surprise then perhaps you would stand a fighting chance, but I've just traced your position using the signal from your phone and have let Colonel Ron know exactly where you are. Good-bye, Clan of the Scorpion. It's been *ice* knowing you."

The phone line went dead.

# CHAPTER SEVEN

## A TRAIL OF LIZARDS' TAILS

As the phone call ended, Donnie heard movement behind him. He turned to find five seals had crept up on him. He spun around once more to find five more seals ahead of him in the tunnel. All of them were spinning ice balls on their noses.

"So you're just a bunch of the Ringmaster's cronies," said Donnie. "He'll have you working in his big top before long."

"We're no one's cronies," barked Colonel Ron, squeezing through the line. "He is helping us and we are helping him.

The rest of my team is starting the timers on the snow explosives as we speak. But before we get out of here, we do have time to practice our aim. Ready, boys, and . . . fire!"

The seals flipped their ice balls into the air, then headed them at Donnie.

Donnie ducked to avoid one, skidded across the ice, and rolled out of the way of another. He flipped up onto his feet and dodged two more that flew past his head and smashed against the wall of the tunnel. He hastily pressed a button on the side of his backpack and an umbrella shot up, sheltering him from the ice that rained down from the smashed ice ball.

The seals stared in confusion.

"Well don't just stand there! Reload!" yelled Colonel Ron.

Donnie pulled two smoke grenades from the harness across his chest and launched

them in opposite directions. Green smoke
poured from the exploded grenades, filling
the chamber.

"Where's he gone?" cried a seal.

"I can't see him!"

"Keep firing!" shouted Colonel Ron.

More ice balls flew in all directions.

"Ow!" cried one of the seals.

"Watch where you're firing," shouted
another.

Donnie didn't waste a second of the
chaos that followed. He slipped on a pair of
specially-designed goggles that enabled
him to see through the dense green smoke
and hurried out of the tunnel.

● ● ●

Meanwhile, the rest of the Clan were making sense of their conversation with the Ringmaster.

"So that's why the clowns ran away," said Jet. "The snow explosives could go off at any minute!"

"I must take a moment to contemplate the nature of this problem," said Chuck.

He sat down cross-legged, closed his eyes, and hummed quietly.

"We haven't got time for this," said Jet. "We have to find Grandmaster One-Eye and get out of here, not sit around with our eyes closed!"

"We have spoken about your impetuous nature before, Jet," replied Chuck, opening one of his eyes. "There are many tunnels in this mountain. We could too easily take

the wrong turn and waste valuable time.
Very soon, these caves will begin to collapse.
Now, please allow me to concentrate."

Chuck closed his eyes once more.

CRUNCH CRUNCH CRUNCH.

Then opened them again.

"Bruce, please. Can't you avoid eating at
a time of such urgency?"

"Sorry," said Bruce. "Only, I just found this
deep-fried lizard's tail on the ground. Lovely."

"Deep-fried lizard's tail!" exclaimed Jet.
"Bruce, you've cracked it! That's what
Grandmaster One-Eye said he would take
from the banquet. He's left us a clue!"

Chuck smiled. "I sought the answer in
my mind, but Bruce found it with his
stomach. Quickly, Bruce, sniff out the rest."

"With pleasure."

They followed the trail of lizards' tails
along the winding tunnel. Bruce ran on

ahead, greedily gulping down each one.
Chuck and Jet followed as quickly as they
could. Suddenly, Bruce's head appeared
around a corner. "Hurry, I've found him!"

Chuck and Jet sped up and rounded the
corner to find Grandmaster One-Eye lying
inside a cage with his eyes closed.

"Grandmaster!" exclaimed Jet. "Are you
all right? What have they done to you?"

The Grandmaster opened his eyes,
yawned and stretched. "Oh, hello, Jet," he
said, getting to his feet. "I'm fine, thanks—
I must have drifted off. Is it time to go?"

"It is indeed. Bruce, get him out,"
ordered Chuck.

Bruce launched his full weight at the door of the cage, but his efforts were in vain. The meerkats had come across the Ringmaster's special reinforced titanium cages before. They were impossible to break, and this time, where there should have been a lock, the door had been welded shut.

"I could try my Single-Claw Hole Punch," said Jet.

"No," said Chuck. "Such a punch can only be used on solid surfaces. If you used it on these bars, the force of it could kill Grandmaster One-Eye. We need Donnie."

Jet pulled his phone out, but before he had even pressed a button it started to ring. "We were just about to call you," he said, switching on the speakerphone. "We've found Grandmaster One-Eye."

"Good, because we only have three and a half minutes to get out of here," said Donnie.

"What?" Bruce replied.

"I've just found one of the snow explosives, and the timer's been activated."

"Can't you disarm it?" asked Chuck.

"Even if I could, there are nine more of these things. We need to get out now."

"But Grandmaster One-Eye is stuck in a titanium cage," said Jet. "It's ninja-proof. We could carry the whole cage out, but not in three and a half minutes."

"Donnie, do you have something we could use to break it open?" asked Chuck.

"Yes, but there's no time," replied Donnie. "I've checked the coordinates of Grandmaster One-Eye's signal, and it'll take two minutes just for me to get to you."

"So we're supposed to leave him here to get blown up?" exclaimed Bruce.

"*Blown up*," said Donnie thoughtfully. "That's it! Stay where you are."

# CHAPTER EIGHT

## BLOWN UP–
## IN A GOOD WAY!

After what seemed like the longest two minutes in history, Donnie arrived carrying a mound of snow with a small electronic display in the middle. The timer was down to just over a minute.

"You've brought an explosive?" exclaimed Jet.

"No time to explain," panted Donnie. "Jet, I need you to use the Single-Claw Hole Punch."

"Where?"

Donnie pointed at the ground. "Down,"

he said. "We need to put this thing about twenty yards directly below us."

Jet closed his eyes, extended one claw, and hummed, then suddenly punched the ground. The force of the blow tore a hole straight through the ice, creating a deep well.

"Your technique has improved considerably," said Chuck.

"Thanks to Professor Longtooth—he told me that when harnessing one's powers for the Single-Claw Hole Punch, a quiet noise will produce a more powerful punch."

"Good work," said Donnie. He dropped the bomb into the hole and turned to the cage. "Now, Grandmaster One-Eye, stand back and shield your eyes."

He pulled two small pieces of plasticine from his backpack and placed them very carefully at either end of one of the bars.

"What are you doing?" asked Grandmaster One-Eye.

"These cages are strong, but their weakest spots are where the bars have been soldered to the frame." He attached a wire that ran from a small black box and took a few steps back. "These plastic explosives should be enough to disconnect one bar. Cover your ears, everyone. You too, Grandmaster."

He pressed a button on the box. There were two bangs in quick succession and

the metal bar clanged to the ground.

"Well done," said Grandmaster One-Eye, clapping his paws. "May I come out now?"

"No, we're coming in," said Donnie.

"What? We're getting in there?" exclaimed Jet.

"Yes. Bruce, you push the cage over the hole first," ordered Donnie. "Hurry!"

Bruce did so, then the Clan of the Scorpion joined Grandmaster One-Eye inside.

"Would you care to explain your plan?" asked Chuck.

"This cage is made of titanium," said Donnie. "We haven't got time to get out before the snow explosives go off and bring the whole mountain down. But then Jet reminded me that bombs blow things up."

"Ah, yes, I see," said Chuck. "*Up.*"

"Exactly," said Donnie. "As long as there is something to protect us, and about twenty feet of ice between us and the blast, the bomb beneath us should produce enough power to shoot us up and out . . . I think. Ideally, I'd have time to test this theory with a scale model, but given the circumstances . . . Hold tight!"

Suddenly, there was a huge explosion accompanied by a cracking, rushing, echoing noise as the heat from the blast melted the ice and the cage was propelled

upward through the mountain. The
meerkats closed their eyes and clung onto
the bars.

The cage shot out of
the mountain face,
soaring up into the air.
For a brief moment, it
hung in the sky, far
above the icy
landscape.

WHOOSH!

"Well. That wasn't so bad," said Bruce.

Then the cage began to fall. It gathered speed as it went, and landed with a THUMP on the side of the mountain. As it slid down the slope, it was accompanied by twenty tons of snow.

"Another avalanche!" yelped Bruce.

"Ahhhhhh!" all five of them cried.

"Hang on!" shouted Jet, pointing ahead. "Where's the rest of the mountain?"

Donnie reached into his backpack and frantically rifled around as the cage flew over the edge of the cliff and dropped like a lead weight.

"Whoooo-ahhh," yelled the meerkats.

"DON-NIEEE!" yelled Jet. "Do something!"

"Hold on! I've got just the thing!" Donnie bellowed.

He pulled a cord inside his bag. A stream of material flew through the bars of the cage

and opened up into a parachute, pinning
Donnie's bag to the ceiling.

"How very thrilling," said Grandmaster
One-Eye, as they glided down to the ground.

"Well done, Donnie," said Chuck. "We all
owe you our lives."

The cage landed with a thump on a snowy ridge and they all scrambled out.

"Now to find the Ringmaster," said Jet.

"That will have to wait," said Donnie. "I traced his call and checked his location when he tapped into our phone. He was telling the truth about being a long way from here. The west coast of America, as far as I can tell."

"So there's no big fight at the end of this mission," said Jet, disappointed. "But we always have a big fight at the end!"

"Hey, Mr. Black, it's those spies again," said a penguin appearing from behind a ridge.

"Indeed it is, Mr. White," said Mr. Black.

The rest of the Tuxedo Ten appeared over the snowy ridge.

"Looks like you'll get your big fight after all, Jet," said Donnie.

"These penguins are only trying to defend their natural habitat," said Chuck. He turned to the Tuxedo Ten. "We have no wish to fight you."

"We have received information that Colonel Ron has employed additional help and, since you are strangers, basic reasoning leads us to believe that you are in cahoots with the seals," said Mr. Gray.

The meerkats looked blankly at him.

"He means we think you're spies," explained Mr. White.

"Yeah, and that means—" Mr. Black was cut off mid-sentence by two snowballs to the chest, which knocked him off his feet and sent him sliding backwards across the ice. The other penguins squawked and trumpeted furiously.

"Take cover!" cried Chuck.

More snowballs came flying through

the air, bowling the penguins over like pins. The meerkats spun around to see the army of seals accompanied by Grimsby, Sheffield, and Barnie the polar bear coming over the opposite ridge.

"The Tuxedo Ten must accept the authority of the seal army," barked Colonel Ron.

Mr. Black picked himself up. "We have already told you, we are happy to share this land, but we will not be ruled by you no matter who you bring in to help you."

"Don't be foolish now," said Colonel Ron. "I have an entire army, two armed humans, and a bear-knuckle fighter." Barnie let out a ferocious roar. "What exactly do you have?"

"They have us," said Chuck.

"Why are we on their side? They attacked us," Bruce pointed out.

"Because while the penguins understand that this land is big enough to live alongside other species, the seals want to dominate," Chuck explained. "And the Clan of the Scorpion will fight any who seek to dominate others."

Chuck drew his sword, then cried, "Before the Clan each enemy cowers, for now we fight till victory is ours!" He led the charge toward the army. Donnie lobbed a handful of smoke grenades at the clowns so they misfired, sending the snowballs harmlessly over the meerkats' heads.

Grandmaster One-Eye remained where he was, picking up the misfired snowballs and hurling them straight back.

"Armed battalion, ready, aim . . . fire!" cried the seal sergeant.

Ice balls flew at the meerkats, but were punched away by Bruce, kicked away by Donnie, and shattered by Chuck's sword.

"Penguins, let's get ready to rumble—tuxedo style," shouted Mr. Black.

The penguins dived onto their bellies, building up momentum as they slid across the ice. They sped toward the seals, catching them off guard and jabbing them with their beaks. Jet, meanwhile, had planted himself deep in the ranks of the seals and was causing chaos by spinning, kicking, and punching anything in sight.

While the clowns were occupied with firing snowballs at the penguins, Donnie and Chuck snuck up behind them and kicked the cannons out of their hands. Chuck rested one gun on his shoulder, aiming it at the clowns, while Donnie pulled the trigger, pummeling them with snowballs.

Meanwhile, Bruce found himself face to foot with Barnie the bear. "Looks like it's just you and me," Bruce snarled.

The polar bear roared angrily and raised his fists.

"Bruce Force!" cried Bruce. He shot into the air with his arms outstretched and landed a powerful double-fisted punch on Barnie's nose, causing him to topple over like a falling tree. Then Bruce leaped onto the bear's belly and pummeled his chest with all his might, until Barnie could take it no more. He got to his feet and ran off as fast as he could.

"I guess he couldn't *bear* any more," said Bruce, looking around to see if anyone was there to hear his joke.

No one was.

Barnie wasn't the only one to have accepted defeat. Without their snowball guns, the clowns were running as fast as their huge shoes would allow them through the deep snow. The seals were retreating too, in spite of Colonel Ron's protests. "Come back, you cowards.... We outnumber them four to one.... Victory will still be ours...."

But the seals were barking loudly as they made their way over the ridge. Grandmaster One-Eye hurled a snowball into the side of Colonel Ron's face. "Oh, all right. I know when I'm beaten," he said. He turned and waddled off. "Wait for me!"

"Nice work," said Mr. Black. He sidled up

to Chuck. "I'm sorry we misjudged you. The Tuxedo Ten are in your debt."

"It was an honor to fight by your side," said Chuck, bowing.

"What was that huge white thing?" said Mr. White.

"It's called a polar bear," said Chuck. "And it's a long way from home."

# CHAPTER NINE

## THE PENGUIN BOOGIE-WOOGIE

The meerkats were keen to jump on board the first boat heading north. They were desperate to find out what terrible scheme the Ringmaster was concocting next. And they wanted to get Grandmaster One-Eye back home where he would be safe. But most of all, they wanted to get warm.

The only problem was, the penguins had insisted on throwing them a party and it seemed rude to say no.

As it turned out, the Tuxedo Ten were excellent hosts. They provided a feast of snow cones, ice cream, and more fish than even Bruce could eat. There were games and races, and the meerkats discovered that the penguins liked to make music, too. They kept the beat with their webbed feet and trumpeted tunes as loudly as they could.

"These penguins are really good," said Bruce. "They should be in show business."

"Don't you mean *snow* business?" asked Donnie.

The others groaned.

"I still wish I had got to fight the Ringmaster," said Jet.

Chuck smiled. "We escaped from a deadly trap and helped these penguins defend their home. I think that is enough for one day."

"Yeah, but who knows what he has planned next?"

"We will find out what he is up to soon enough. And when we do, I guarantee our appearance will come as an unpleasant—as well as unexpected—surprise," Chuck assured him.

"Talking of unexpected, take a look over there," said Donnie.

Grandmaster One-Eye was standing in the middle of a crowd of trumpeting penguins, spinning in circles and moving his hips, using his walking stick for balance.

"What on earth is he doing?" asked Jet. "He'll make himself dizzy."

"I believe he's breakdancing," said Chuck.
"Isn't he a bit old for that?" said Bruce.
The ancient meerkat noticed them
looking and called over. "Hey, it's just like
the old days. I've still got it!"

"Well, whatever 'it' is, I just hope it's
not contagious," chuckled Donnie.

# GO**FISH**

**Gareth P. Jones**

**What did you want to be
when you grew up?**
At various points, a writer, a mu-
sician, an intergalactic bounty
hunter and, for a limited period,
a graphic designer. (I didn't know
what that meant, but I liked the way it sounded.)

**When did you realize you wanted to be a writer?**
I don't remember realizing it. I have always loved stories. From a very young age, I enjoyed making them up.
As I'm not very good at making things up on the spot,
this invariably involved having to write them down.

**What's your most embarrassing childhood
memory?**
Seriously? There are too many. I have spent my entire
life saying and doing embarrassing things. Just thinking
about some of them is making me cringe. Luckily, I have
a terrible memory, so I can't remember them all, but no,
I'm not going to write any down for you. If I did that, I'd
never be able to forget them.

 SQUARE FISH

**What's your favorite childhood memory?**
To be honest with you, I don't remember my childhood very well at all (I told you I had a bad memory), but I do recall how my dad used to tell me stories. He would make them up as he went along, most likely borrowing all sorts of elements from the books he was reading without me knowing.

**As a young person, who did you look up to most?**
My mom and dad, Prince, Michael Jackson, all of Monty Python, and Stephen Fry.

**What was your favorite thing about school?**
Laughing with my friends.

**What was your least favorite thing about school?**
I had a bit of a hard time when I moved from the Midlands to London at the age of twelve because I had a funny accent. But don't worry, it was all right in the end.

**What were your hobbies as a kid? What are your hobbies now?**
I love listening to and making music. My hobbies haven't really changed over the years, except that there's a longer list of instruments now. When I get a chance, I like idling away the day playing trumpet, guitar, banjo, ukulele, mandolin (and piano if there's one in the vicinity). I also like playing out with my friends.

## What was your first job, and what was your "worst" job?

My first job was working as a waiter. That's probably my worst job, too. As my dad says, I was a remarkably grumpy waiter. I'm not big on all that serving-people malarkey.

## What book is on your nightstand now?

I have a pile of books from my new publisher. I'm trying to get through them before I meet the authors. I'm halfway through *Maggot Moon* by Sally Gardner, which is written in the amazing voice of a dyslexic boy.

## How did you celebrate publishing your first book?

The first time I saw one of my books in a shop, I was so excited that I caused something of a commotion. I managed to persuade an unsuspecting customer to buy it so I could sign it for her son.

## Where do you write your books?

Anywhere and everywhere. Here are some of the locations I have written the Ninja Meerkats series: On the 185 and the 176 buses in London, various airplanes, Hong Kong, Melbourne, all over New Zealand, a number of cafes and bars between San Diego and San Francisco, New Quay in South Wales, and my kitchen.

## What sparked your imagination for *The Ninja Meerkats*?

The idea came from the publishing house, but from the moment I heard it, I really wanted to write it. It reminded me of lots of action-packed cartoons I used to watch when I was young. I love the fact that I get to cram in lots of jokes and puns, fast action, and crazy outlandish plots.

**The Ninja Meerkats are awesome fighters; have you ever studied martial arts? If so, what types?**
Ha, no. If I was to get into a fight, my tactic would be to fall over and hope that whoever was attacking me lost interest.

**If you were a Ninja Meerkat, what would your name be?**
Hmm, how about Gareth *POW!* Jones?

**What's your favorite exhibit or animal at the zoo?**
Funnily enough, I like the meerkats. I was at a zoo watching them the other day when it started to rain. They suddenly ran for cover, looking exactly like their human visitors.

**What's Bruce's favorite food?**
Anything with the words ALL YOU CAN EAT written above it.

**If you had a catchphrase like Bruce Force! or Ninja-Boom! what would it be?**
That's a tricky one. How about PEN POWER!

**If you were a Ninja Meerkat, what would your special ninja skill be?**
I like to think I'd be like Jet, and always working on a new one. When I got into school, I took the Random Move

Generator! We used it to come up with new moves, like the Floating Butterfly Punch and the Ultimate Lemon Punch.

**What is your favorite thing about real-life meerkats? Have you ever met a meerkat?**
I was lucky enough to go into a meerkat enclosure recently. They were crawling all over me, trying to get a good view. It was brilliant.

**What challenges do you face in the writing process, and how do you overcome them?**
The challenge with writing the Ninja Meerkats books is mostly about the plotting. It's trying to get all the twists and turns to work, and to avoid them feeling predictable. When I hit problems, I write down as many options as I can think of from the completely ordinary to utterly ridiculous. Once they're all down on paper, the right answer normally jumps out at you.

**Which of your characters is most like you?**
I'd like to say that I'm wise and noble like Chuck, but I'm probably more like the Ringmaster as we're both always coming up with new ways to take over the world.

**What makes you laugh out loud?**
My friends.

**What do you do on a rainy day?**
Play guitar, write, watch TV, or go out with my sword-handled umbrella.

**What's your idea of fun?**
Answering questionnaires about myself. Actually, tomorrow, I'm going to a music festival with my wife where we will dance and cavort. That should be fun.

**What's your favorite song?**
There are far too many to mention, but today I think I'll go for "Feel Good Inc." by Gorillaz.

**Who is your favorite fictional character?**
Another tricky one, but today I'll say Ged from the Earthsea Trilogy by Ursula K. Le Guin.

**What was your favorite book when you were a kid? Do you have a favorite book now?**
As a child, I especially loved *The Phantom Tollbooth* by Norton Juster.

**What's your favorite TV show or movie?**
*Raiders of the Lost Ark.*

**If you were stranded on a desert island, who would you want for company?**
My wife and son, then probably my friend Pete, as he's really handy and would be able to make and build things.

**If you could travel anywhere in the world, where would you go and what would you do?**
I'd like to go to Canada next. Ideally, I'd like to go and live there for a bit. I've never been to South America. There are also lots of parts of America I haven't visited yet.

**If you could travel in time, where would you go and what would you do?**
I think I'd travel to the future and see what's changed and whether anyone's invented a new kind of umbrella.

**What's the best advice you have ever received about writing?**
Don't tell the story, show the story.

**What advice do you wish someone had given you when you were younger?**
Everything's probably going to be fine, so it's best to enjoy yourself.

**Do you ever get writer's block? What do you do to get back on track?**
It feels like tempting fate, but I don't really believe in writer's block. I think if you can't write, you're doing the wrong thing. You may need to plan or jot down options or go for a walk.

**What do you want readers to remember about your books?**
I'd settle for a general feeling of having enjoyed them.

**What would you do if you ever stopped writing?**
I'd do a full stop. If this is for an American audience, I guess that would be a period.

**What should people know about you?**
I'm a very silly man.

SQUARE FISH

**What do you like best about yourself?**
I'm a very silly man.

**Do you have any strange or funny habits? Did you when you were a kid?**
I talk to myself a lot, which is probably pretty common, but the difference is that I don't listen to what I'm saying.

Hollywood has a new STAR, Doris the Dancing Dog, but the meerkats are convinced that the evil Ringmaster is behind her newfound fame. Will the meerkats be able to figure out his evil plot in time?

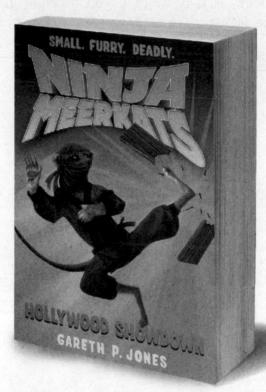

Find out what happens in

# Ninja Meerkats:
# Hollywood Showdown

# CHAPTER ONE

## OLD DOGS, NEW TRICKS

Hundreds of planes arrive at Los Angeles International Airport every day, bringing tourists from around the world to the city. They come to soak up sunshine, glamour, and excitement, and to visit the city's most famous district: Hollywood. It was on one such plane that Chuck, Donnie, Jet, and Bruce (otherwise known as the Clan of the Scorpion) had arrived, hidden in an overhead luggage compartment. They were now making their way across the airport arrivals hall, heading for the exit.

You might think that four ninja meerkats walking through a bustling airport would cause something of a stir. But the Clan moved around undetected, thanks to one of Donnie's cunning disguises. As far as humans were concerned, all they could see was a child in a pair of baggy jeans and a hoodie. Inside the outfit, however, were four meerkats balanced on each other's shoulders.

Bruce Willowhammer, the strongest of the team, was at the bottom of the pile, and had his furry feet strapped to a pair of stilts. On his shoulders were Jet Flashfeet and Donnie Dragonjab, whose trademark bag of gadgets was strapped to his back. Jet and Donnie were each operating one of the child disguise's arms, opening doors, pressing elevator buttons and, at one point, batting away an over-friendly dog. At the top of the

stack was Chuck Cobracrusher, the leader of
the group, his face hidden
inside the hooded top.

The only problem
with this arrangement
was that it
meant Bruce
was in control
of where the Clan went.

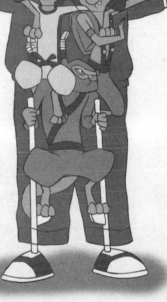

And Bruce was easily
distracted.

As he strode across
the arrivals hall, he
peered through a pair of
eyeholes at the top
of the jeans. "Hey, that's
Vin Pain!" he exclaimed,
spotting a TV screen showing an
entertainment news program. He quickly
changed direction and headed for the TV.

"Bruce, remember our mission," warned Chuck. "We need to find out where the Ringmaster is, and what he is up to!"

"Who's Vin Pain?" asked Jet, folding down a specially designed pocket flap in the hoodie so he could see the TV, too.

"Sounds like something you'd tell the doctor about," said Donnie. "Ooh, I've got a nasty Vin Pain all down my back."

"Who's Vin Pain?" exclaimed Bruce. "Only the best action hero in the world, that's who! Haven't you seen *Blown to Pieces*? What about *The Smash-Up Man* or *Big Guns and Loud Bangs*? Brilliant films. Some of them are really clever, too."

The TV showed a clip from a film in which Vin Pain was jumping across the tops of cars hurtling down a busy highway, while dodging a storm of bullets that rained down on him from a helicopter.

"Yeah, looks *really* clever," said Donnie sarcastically.

"Bruce, we do not have time to watch TV right now. We need to keep moving," Chuck called down.

"Vin does all his own stunts and everything," said Bruce, ignoring Chuck.

"Ha," snorted Jet. "I bet he can't do a Super Looping Somersault Leap. That's my new move. I read about it in *How to Flatten Your Enemies and Beat People*."

"Shhh!" said Bruce. "Vin's about to say his trademark line."

On the screen, a building burst into flames for no good reason. Standing in front of it, the muscle-bound star turned to the camera and said in a gruff voice, "Things are getting rough around here... so I'm about to get tough."

"Brilliant," said Bruce, clapping his paws excitedly, causing the others to wobble precariously above him.

Chuck tutted. "The Way of the Scorpion teaches us not to engage in such showy displays. Calmness and serenity are our goals. We should only lift a paw to fight when we have no other choice."

"Actually, that was pretty cool, Chuck," said Jet.

"Why does everything always burst into flames in Hollywood films?" sighed Donnie.

On the TV, a female reporter with alarmingly white teeth filled the screen.

"Action hero Vin Pain is used to saying how things are *getting rough*, but in Vin's next film it's a case of things *going woof*." She smirked, then continued. "Why? Because Vin's new co-star is a dog. Her name? Doris the Dancing Dog." The screen showed the familiar face of Doris, the Ringmaster's faithful canine companion.

"So, Doris is a movie star now," said Chuck. "Most interesting . . ."

The picture changed to show Doris having her photo taken alongside Vin Pain on the red carpet at a film premiere.

"The film's title is a closely guarded secret and very little is known about the canine newcomer," continued the reporter, "except that she is currently being trained at the Real Academy of Dog Actors, or RADA for short. The acting school is run by celebrity dog trainer Honor Longlead, who joins us now."

The TV showed another smiling woman with equally white teeth.

"So, Honor," said the reporter, "is Doris the Dancing Dog a superstar in the making?"

"Absolutely. Doris is a very talented pup," she replied. "She's been circus trained, but you should see her during the fight scenes. She's a natural."

"I bet she is," muttered Jet. The Clan of the Scorpion had come up against Doris on more than one occasion and had the scars to prove it.

"Well, we look forward to seeing her in action! Thanks, Honor. That's it for this week's edition of *Hollywood Spotlight*. Or should I say, *Holly*woof *Spotlight*?" The presenter smiled and moved on to the next item. "Coming up after the break, we'll be discussing why the U.S. president flew into L.A. this morning along with his super-cute pet sausage dog, Chip O'Lata. Some are saying it's a popularity-boosting trip before the beginning of election season next month. . . ."

Bruce turned away from the screen and headed for the exit.

"Well, Bruce, it would appear that your love of film has given us our first lead," said Chuck, "and it is a *dog* lead. We will head straight for this acting school. The Ringmaster is sure to be behind Doris's newfound fame, so he won't be far away. . . ."

"Can we go and see where Vin made *Dynamite for Dinner* later? And the sequel, *Destruction for Dessert?*" asked Bruce.

"Once we have defeated the Ringmaster, perhaps," Chuck replied. "Until then, we must be like movie cameras, and stay focused."